HULK™

The Beast Within

UNIVERSAL PICTURES PRESENTS IN ASSOCIATION WITH MARVEL ENTERPRISES A VALHALLA MOTION PICTURES / GOOD MACHINE PRODUCTION AN ANG LEE FILM "THE HULK"
ERIC BANA JENNIFER CONNELLY SAM ELLIOTT JOSH LUCAS AND NICK NOLTE MUSIC BY MYCHAEL DANNA COSTUME DESIGNER MARIT ALLEN EDITOR TIM SQUYRES ACE PRODUCTION DESIGNER RICK HEINRICHS
DIRECTOR OF PHOTOGRAPHY FREDERICK ELMES ASC EXECUTIVE PRODUCERS STAN LEE KEVIN FEIGE PRODUCED BY GALE ANNE HURD AVI ARAD JAMES SCHAMUS LARRY FRANCO WRITTEN BY JAMES SCHAMUS DIRECTED BY ANG LEE
MARVEL THIS FILM IS NOT YET RATED SPECIAL VISUAL EFFECTS AND ANIMATION BY INDUSTRIAL LIGHT & MAGIC www.thehulk.com A UNIVERSAL PICTURE UNIVERSAL

The Hulk™: The Beast Within
HarperCollins®, ®, and HarperFestival® are trademarks of HarperCollins Publishers Inc.

Library of Congress catalog card number: 2002115898
1 2 3 4 5 6 7 8 9 10
❖
First Edition
www.harperchildrens.com
www.thehulk.com

The Beast Within

Adapted by Scout Driggs
Based on the motion picture screenplay
by James Schamus

HarperFestival®
A Division of HarperCollins*Publishers*

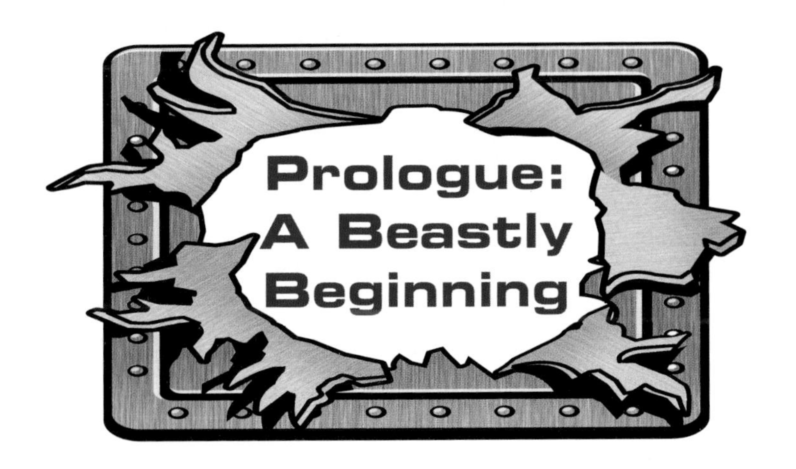

Prologue: A Beastly Beginning

This is a story of man and beast, a tale of hero and monster. This is the story of Bruce Banner.

Sure, Bruce may seem like a normal guy. He has a regular job. He lives in a regular house. He even has a girlfriend—sort of. But this mild-mannered scientist isn't ordinary at all.

You see, Bruce Banner was born with a secret—a secret so dangerous it could destroy him; a secret that causes him to transform into the most powerful creature ever to walk the earth—the Hulk!

The story of the Hulk begins thirty years ago. In fact, it starts before Bruce Banner was even born. This story begins with another young scientist—Bruce Banner's father, David Banner. . . .

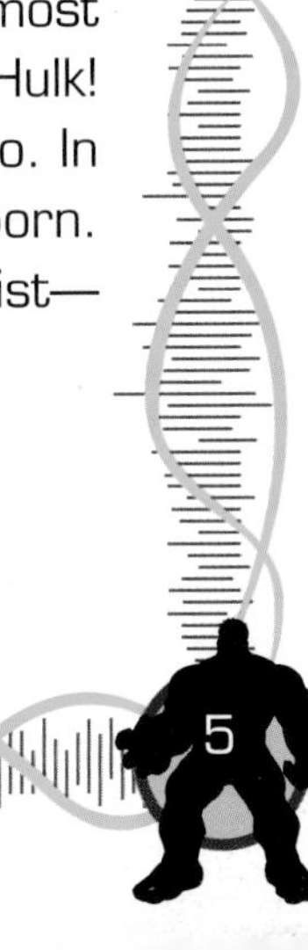

The Making of a Monster

"There is simply no way to shield against every weaponized agent," young David Banner explained to Thaddeus "Thunderbolt" Ross. "Instead, I can make superimmune systems."

The superimmune system was new technology that, once perfected, would allow people to instantly heal themselves. It would be like a superhealing power! Cuts on your skin would magically seal up. Broken bones could attach back together seamlessly.

Ross thought David's research was too risky.

"Banner, I know what you're doing," said Ross accusingly. "Manipulating the immune system is dangerous. I've told you a hundred times—no human subjects!"

But David desperately wanted to test his theory on a real person. He wasn't about to let Ross stop him from the most important project of his life.

So David decided to ignore Ross's orders. When the lab was empty, David injected himself with mutagenic agents. The agents were designed to reconstruct his immune system. Now he would be able to test his superimmune system without anyone ever finding out.

David knew it was a risky choice. What he didn't know was that this decision would haunt him for the rest of his life.

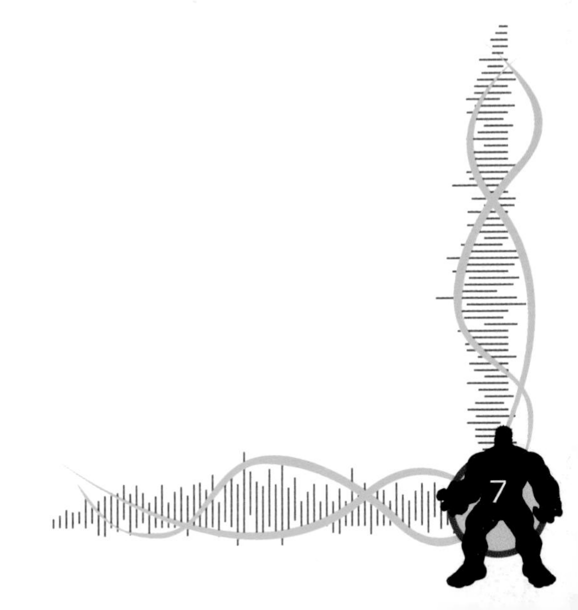

A Beast Is Born

"David, I have wonderful news," said Edith Banner excitedly. "We're going to have a baby!"

David stared back at his wife in horror. *A baby!* All he could think about was the secret experiment, the mutagenic agents. Could these agents be passed along genetically? What would mutant cells do to an unborn baby?

But when Bruce was born, he appeared quite normal—mostly. There was one strange thing: Whenever Bruce became angry his body would bulge and swell. Then suddenly it would stop. With enormous effort, little Bruce seemed able to control it. Whatever *it* was.

David studied Bruce suspiciously. He knew there was something unnatural going on inside his son.

Sabotage

Four years had passed. "The blood samples we found in your lab were human blood," said Ross, accusingly. "You've ignored protocol."

"You had no right to go snooping around my lab," yelled David. "That's my business!"

"Wrong, Banner," shouted Ross. "It's government business. And you're off the project!"

David became furious. Something snapped inside him. He went out of his mind.

Shaking with rage, David flipped a series of switches. Alarms began to sound.

* * *

The Banners lived in a house at the Desert Base, where David's lab was. They were so close that the shrieking alarm pulsed through the Banner's home. On the living room floor, little Bruce was playing with his toys. David entered the house

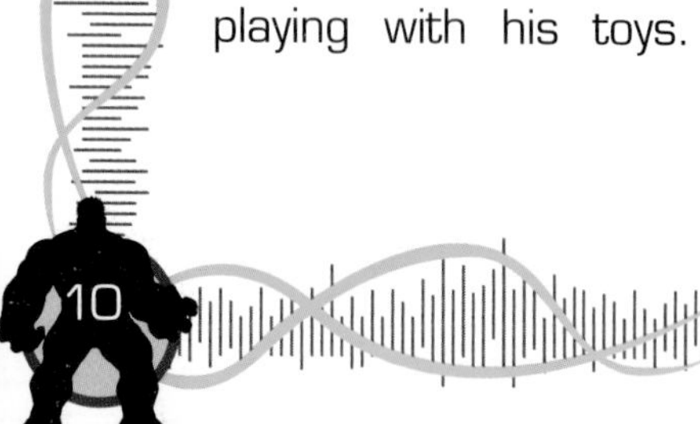

abruptly and began arguing with Edith. Bruce watched his parents fight as alarms continued to bellow in the distance. He could tell that something was very wrong.

Suddenly a flash of light—Bruce looked up—then a scream . . .

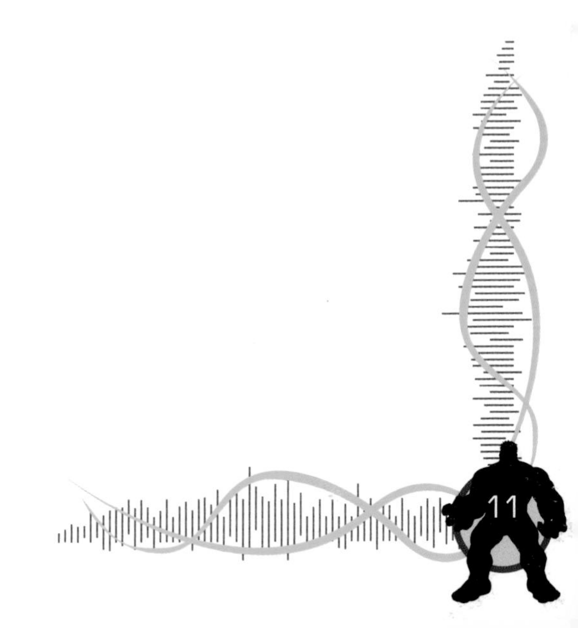

A Glimpse of Green

It was now ten years later. An elderly woman rushed down the hallway toward a loud scream. She opened the door and flipped on the light.

Fourteen-year-old Bruce stared blankly. He now believed his name was Bruce Krenzler. He had no memory of his early childhood.

"Another nightmare, Bruce?" asked Mrs. Krenzler, his adoptive mother.

"I don't know. I can't remember," he replied.

Later at school, Bruce was looking through the eye of a microscope in the science lab. A beautiful girl named Alice approached him. Bruce noticed her, and began to blush. He was not very good with girls. Actually, Bruce didn't have many friends at all. He liked to keep to himself, keep hidden.

"Hi, Bruce. Whatcha doing?" asked Alice.

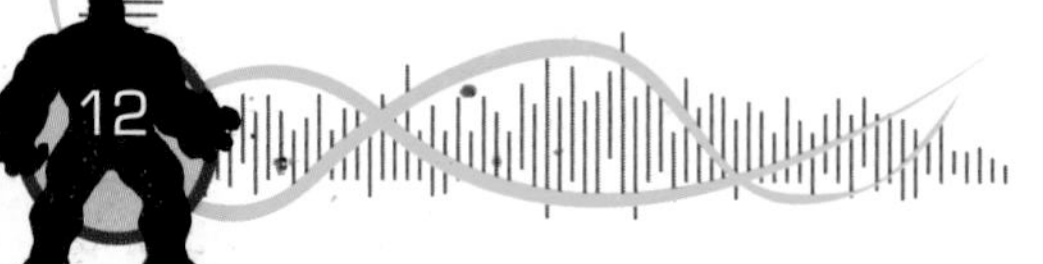

"This is cool. Uh, you can check out the DNA," Bruce stammered. "You know, the proteins."

Alice leaned in to see. "You know," she said, "I really like brainy guys."

Alice moved closer to Bruce. He stepped back awkwardly and fell over a stool.

Suddenly there was laughter everywhere. A group of students had been watching them the whole time. It was a setup. They were trying to make Bruce look stupid.

"Poor Bruce," said Alice. "You sure are a nerd."

Without warning Bruce's face erupted with anger. A powerful force was unleashed, causing his entire body to shake. Bruce grabbed the side of the table and held himself up. His body convulsed so badly that everything on the table scattered. A lit Bunsen burner fell to the ground, and a small fire began to spread as the students ran screaming from the room.

* * *

Four more years had passed. Bruce was in his room reading. Science books were scatter the floor all around him. Mrs. Krenzler ent room and sat down beside him.

"Hey, Mom," said Bruce.

"Bruce, you're almost off to coll

Krenzler sadly. "I am going to miss you terribly. But someday you will be a remarkable scientist."

"Like my father?" asked Bruce.

"Do you remember him?" Mrs. Krenzler wondered.

"No, but you said once that he was a scientist," explained Bruce.

"Did I?" asked Mrs. Krenzler, a bit taken aback. "I must have been guessing, seeing how brilliant you are," she said, covering her tracks.

"Someday you will discover there is something inside you, something special, a kind of greatness," continued Mrs. Krenzler. "Someday you will share it with the whole world."

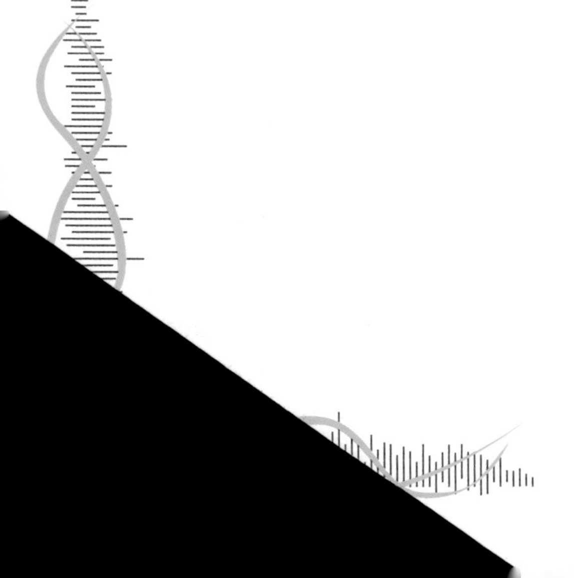

All Grown Up

Thirty-year-old Bruce Krenzler stood in front of the bathroom mirror. As he shaved his chin, Bruce felt a strange but familiar sensation. When he looked into his eyes, it felt as if someone else was looking back at him—watching him. It was creepy.

Later, at the government lab where he worked, Bruce conducted an experiment. Large bulging eyes looked at him. This time they were the eyes of a frog. The frog unwittingly sat trapped inside a chamber of thick glass. Surrounding the glass were the glittering panels of the gammasphere.

"Harper, release the nanomeds," instructed Bruce. With a low hissing sound, the chamber holding the frog filled with gas.

"Okay, let's hit it with the gamma radiation," said Bruce. Harper, the lab assistant, punched instructions onto a keyboard.

In a flash a small amount of radiation zapped

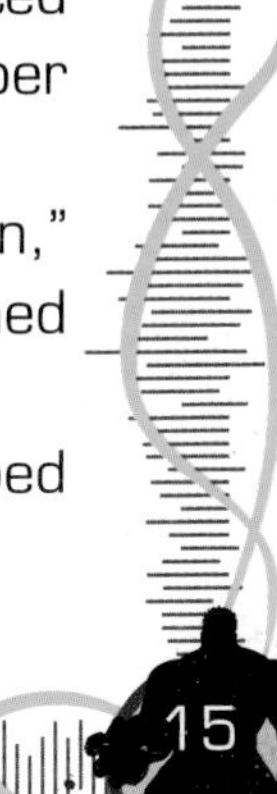

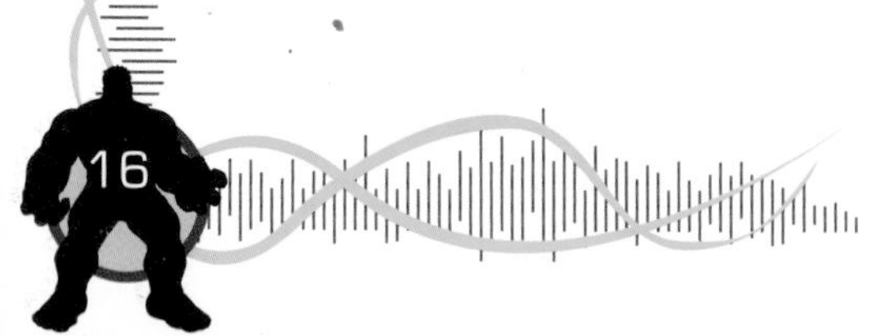

the frog across the belly. A huge cut burst open.

Then, incredibly, the wound began to close up. As it did, it left an area of throbbing green tissue.

"Yes!" Betty Ross, Bruce's colleague and former girlfriend, said under her breath.

Suddenly—*Splat!*—the frog exploded!

The scientists were working on new technology that would trigger instant body repair. But so far no living creature had been able to survive their research.

Bruce and Betty looked down with disappointment. The experiment had failed again.

Bruce packed his bag and headed home for the night. As he walked toward the door he heard something strange. It sounded like a whimpering dog.

Turning the corner, Bruce saw a white mangy-looking poodle. "Hey there, who are you?" asked Bruce as he reached down to pet the dog.

"Grrrrr!" went the poodle as it snapped its rotten teeth at him.

"OK, OK," said Bruce, as he backed away from the mean animal. *I wonder where its owner is?* he thought as he walked out.

Back inside, a janitor lingered near Bruce's lab. There was something unusual about this man.

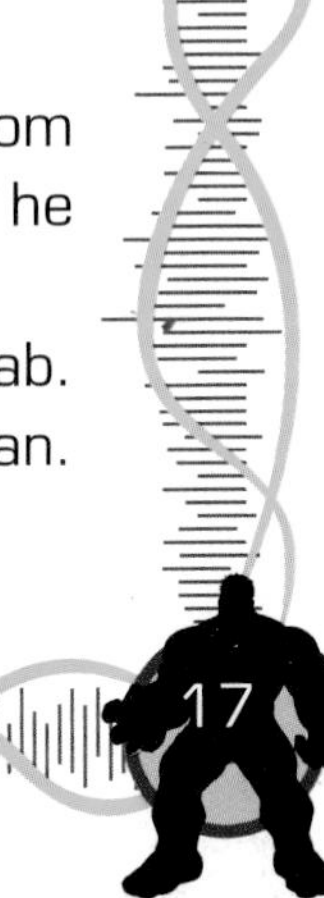

Bruce and Betty had both noticed him lurking around, watching them. But neither of them had really thought too much about it.

The janitor entered the lab quietly and sat down in Bruce's chair. His hand rubbed the chair lovingly.

The janitor found a dark hair and held it up to the light. The hair belonged to Bruce.

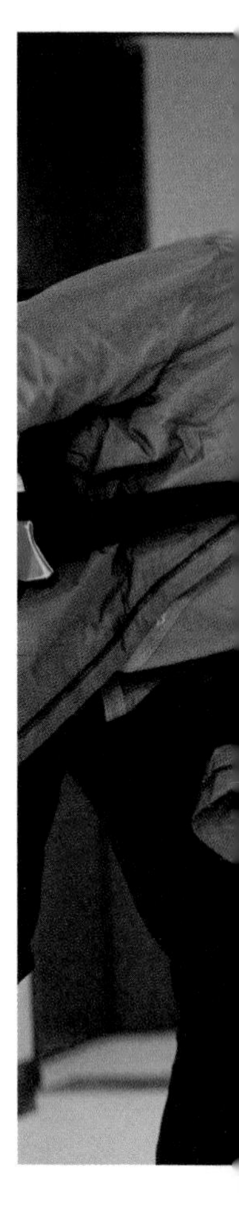

A Father Returns

The janitor walked up to a small house with a run-down yard. He opened the gate and three dogs ran in ahead of him.

The house was filthy. There wasn't much furniture—a mattress, a table, and a chair. A single lightbulb hung from the ceiling. The table was covered with papers, books, a laptop computer, and a microscope.

The man sat at the table and turned on the computer. The man was David Banner—Bruce Banner's long-lost father!

From a small container in his pocket, David pulled out a strand of hair. It was the same hair he had taken from the lab. He was going to study Bruce's DNA.

David placed the hair under a microscope. He couldn't believe what he saw. Finally he understood what lay silent inside of Bruce.

The Enemy

As Bruce entered the lab the next day, he saw Betty talking to Glen Talbot. Glen was an old friend of Betty's who worked as a scientist for a company that was subcontracted by the government. Actually, Glen worked for Betty's father, "Thunderbolt" Ross, who was now a very important general.

Glen came to get information about Bruce and Betty's research. He wanted to take over the project.

"What's he doing here?" Bruce asked angrily.

"You know, Bruce, we've never really gotten a chance to know each other properly," replied Glen.

"That's because I don't want to get to know you properly—or improperly. Leave!" demanded Bruce.

Bruce knew what Glen had planned. He would never let him take over his research.

The Awakening

"Okay, fifteen seconds. We're set for double exposure," said Harper, as he initiated the experiment. But then the computer screen started blinking, and the countdown stopped.

"Hey, Harper. Is there a problem?" asked Bruce.

"The interlock switch flaked again," replied Harper. "It'll be just a sec." Harper grabbed a respirator mask and entered the gammasphere chamber.

"Um, I think the circuit is kind of fried," said Harper over the intercom. "You want to take a look?"

"Okay, hold on," Bruce said as he too picked up a respirator mask. Just as Bruce entered the gammasphere chamber, the interlock switch shorted out with a spark. Suddenly the countdown resumed!

Harper tried to back out of the room, but his respirator mask caught on a rod sticking out of the wall. He began to panic.

Fortunately for Harper, Bruce freed the snagged mask. Harper sprinted out of the chamber.

Out in the control room, Betty tried to stop the countdown. But she couldn't do anything —the monitor and the keyboard were both frozen!

"Bruce!" Betty screamed. "The interlock!" Bruce was now trapped with no way out.

Just then the countdown reached zero. The nanomeds released as the gamma canisters turned to fire blasts of radiation. Bruce quickly realized that Harper and Betty were directly in the line of fire. He turned back to the gammasphere, raised his arms, and blocked the opening with his body.

The gamma canisters fired. Bruce took the full blast. His body glowed green with radiation.

Bruce let out a terrible scream as he fell to his knees.

C32
A15
A19

A Father Revealed

Later that day, Betty entered the emergency room. "I'm going to be OK," Bruce said, looking a little shaky. "Really, barely enough radiation for a slight tan."

"We're still checking," the doctor told Betty. "According to the radiation badge he was wearing, your friend should be burnt toast right now. But I can't find much of anything."

Betty couldn't believe what she had just heard. If this was true, it meant that Bruce was the first person or creature ever to survive their experiment. He had been exposed to enough gamma radiation to kill a thousand men—but he survived!

* * *

Bruce woke with a start. He looked across the hospital room and saw a man sitting in the dark surrounded by dogs. Bruce recognized him as the janitor from the lab.

Bruce sat up in the bed. There was something strangely familiar about the man, yet at the same time, he seemed dangerous.

"Your name is not Krenzler," said the man. "It's Banner."

"What?" asked Bruce.

"Your name. It's Banner, Bruce Banner," he continued.

The man told Bruce he could help him understand why he survived the radiation blast—and why Bruce had always felt something strange inside him.

"You don't want to believe it, but I can see it in your eyes—so much like your mother's," confessed the man. "Of course you're my flesh and blood—but then you're something else too, aren't you?"

Bruce didn't know what to think. What was this stranger talking about? "You're lying. My parents died when I was a young boy."

"That's what they wanted you to believe," the man told Bruce. "The experiments, the accident—they were top secret. They put me away for thirty years." He continued his incredible story: "You see, everything your extraordinary mind has been seeking all these years—it's been inside of you. Now we will understand it, harness it."

"You're crazy, get out!" Bruce screamed, confused and angry.

A look of hostility swept across the man's face. The dogs crouched for attack. "Heel," he commanded. The dogs backed off.

"You're going to have to watch that temper," said the man, David Banner, as he turned to leave.

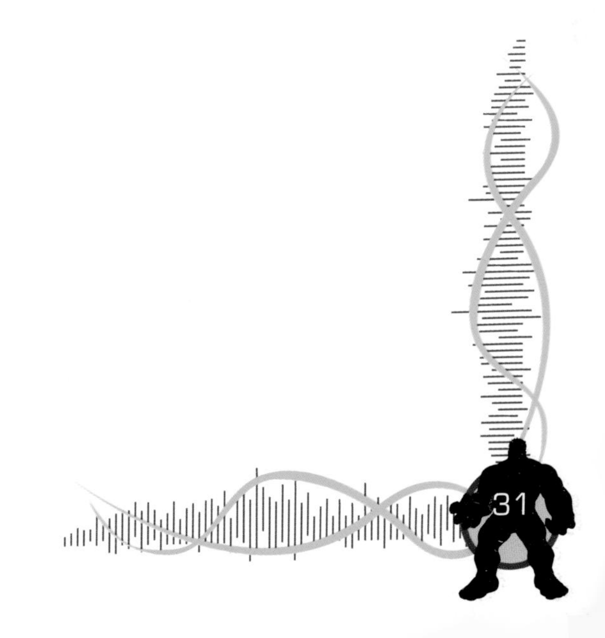

Things That Go Bump in the Night

Bruce tossed and turned in the hospital bed. Under the sheets his body bulged and stretched. The intravenous tubes popped out from the pressure. His eyes turned a greenish color. For a moment he looked like a monster!

Before he knew what had happened, Bruce woke up. He stumbled in the darkness to the bathroom and looked at himself in the mirror.

At first he didn't notice anything unusual—but then, he saw his clothes. They were ripped at the seams! It was almost as though his body had grown right out of them.

Bruce was very afraid. Had the gamma radiation triggered something inside him?

* * *

When Bruce was released from the hospital he headed straight for the lab. He wanted to examine his blood for possible answers. Bruce didn't want to believe what the stranger had told him.

Bruce placed a sample of his blood under the microscope. *The cells,* thought Bruce, *chemical bonds in the DNA . . . storing too much energy . . . impossible . . . impossible.*

Just then the phone rang. The answering machine picked up. "Bruce?" It was Betty. "I saw my father. We had lunch today—it's like he suspects you of something," she said frantically into the machine. "I think they're planning something with the lab, with you."

General Ross, Betty's father, had found out Bruce's true identity and planned to keep him away from the lab—and Betty—forever.

Bruce jumped up to answer the phone before Betty hung up. He knocked the vial of blood off the table, spilling the dark liquid onto the floor. He looked at the blood, horrified. *What am I?* he wondered.

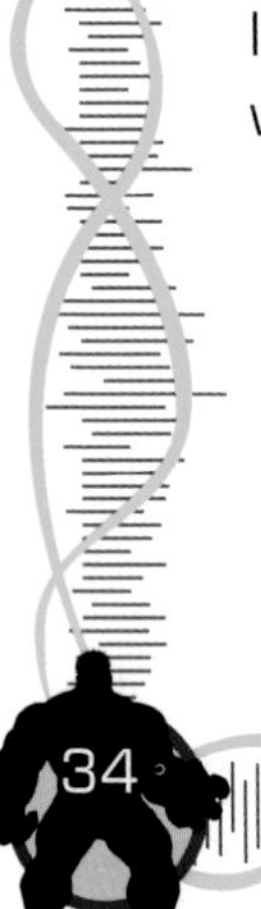

The Hulk Is Here

Bruce heard the whimpering dog again. He ran out of the lab toward the sound. He wanted to find the stranger. Maybe Bruce needed his help after all.

As Bruce turned a corner he smashed into an equipment cart in the hallway. *Ouch!* But he kept running, desperately searching for answers. *Bam!* He tripped and hit the wall. His lip began to swell and bleed.

Bruce lifted himself off the floor, and an unearthly cry emerged from his mouth. He continued to run down the hall, growing bigger and more powerful by the second. As he exploded out of his clothes, his fury destroyed everything in its path.

Huge green fists punched through the wall! Enormous green tree-trunk legs ran with amazing speed! Green arms with bulging muscles lifted and threw the gammasphere through the roof!

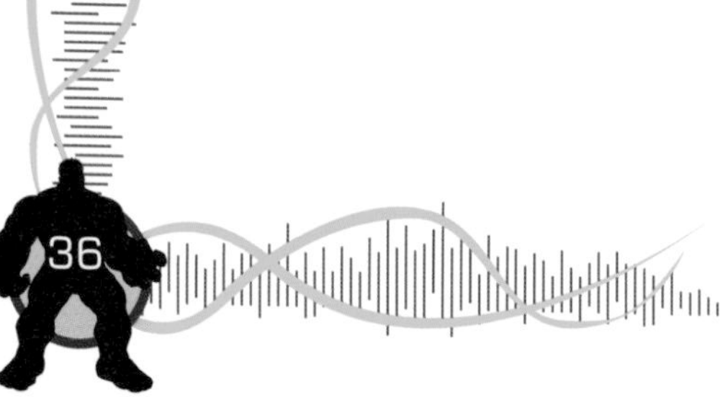

It had finally happened. With the help of the gamma radiation, Bruce unleashed the monster living inside him. In his anger and frustration, he had released the Hulk.

Instinctively, the Hulk's keen eyes noticed someone watching him. It was David Banner, the strange man from the lab. The Hulk jumped up and landed right in front of him.

Oddly, David wasn't scared. He reached out and tenderly touched the hard green flesh. For a moment the Hulk was calmed.

The moment didn't last. The sound of screaming sirens coming closer enraged the Hulk once more. He leaped straight up and tore through the damaged roof. As the police and emergency crew pulled up, all they saw was the huge shadow of a figure merging into the trees.

* * *

Bruce woke up at home the next day. He had no memory of the night before.

A phone was ringing. Bruce picked up the telephone, but it was dead. The ringing continued. He traced the sound to a chair, and under the cushion he found a small cell phone.

"Hello?" said the voice on the other end. It was David Banner.

"What's wrong with me?" asked Bruce. "What did you do to me?"

David told him how he had experimented on himself and unintentionally passed something on to Bruce. "You could call it a deformity," explained David. "But it is an amazing strength too. And now unleashed, I can finally harvest it. As for Betty, I'm sending her a surprise visit from some four-legged friends."

David knew that Bruce, with Betty's help, would try and destroy the monster before it could do any harm. He didn't want that to happen. He wanted to use Bruce's inner powers for himself; he had to protect the Hulk. He had to get rid of Betty.

Earlier, David had collected some DNA from the sample of Bruce's hair. He used it to mutate his dogs. He turned them into raging animal monsters that could destroy anything. And now he sent them after Betty.

Bruce slammed down the phone and headed to the front door. He would save Betty himself. Before he got out the door, however, Glen Talbot showed up.

"Talbot, listen," said Bruce frantically. "It's my father. I think he's going to go after Betty."

But Glen didn't care about Betty. He came to find out what Bruce knew about the green monster that had been sighted at the lab. He wanted to gather information about the Hulk for

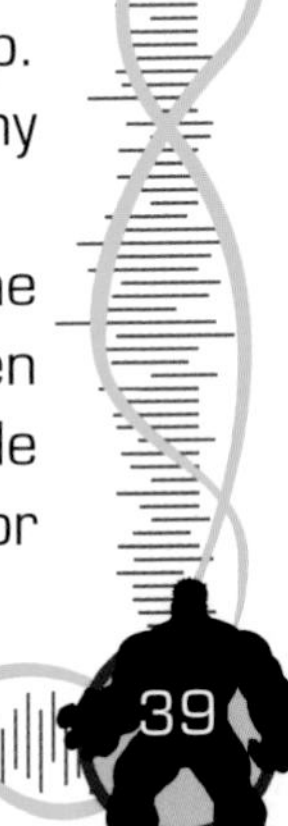

himself. It would be the greatest discovery of any scientist's career.

Talbot entered the house and kicked the door shut. Bruce tried to get past Talbot, but he wouldn't budge. Just then Talbot kicked Bruce's legs out from under him. Bruce fell to the floor with a thud. Talbot pressed his foot to Bruce's chest, pinning him down. He grabbed on to Talbot's leg with both hands. Bruce struggled, but Talbot was too strong.

"You're making me angry," warned Bruce. "I don't think you'd like me when I'm angry."

Talbot smiled and threw a punch at Bruce's stomach. Bruce intercepted the punch and squeezed Talbot's fist. Talbot's face began to tremble and his eyes widened with fear.

Sweat poured from Bruce's face. His body began to strain against his clothes. All of a sudden his face became distorted and turned green. Powerful muscles bulged and grew larger. The raging beast was again released—more powerful, more dangerous, more uncontrollable than before—the Hulk had returned!

With a deafening roar, the Hulk kicked Talbot through a window. Then he simply walked through the front wall of the house and emerged outside.

The military police had escorted Talbot, and were waiting outside. They drew their guns and

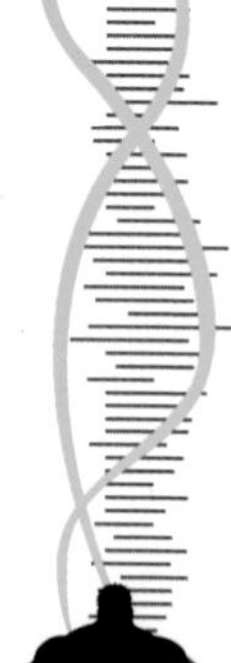

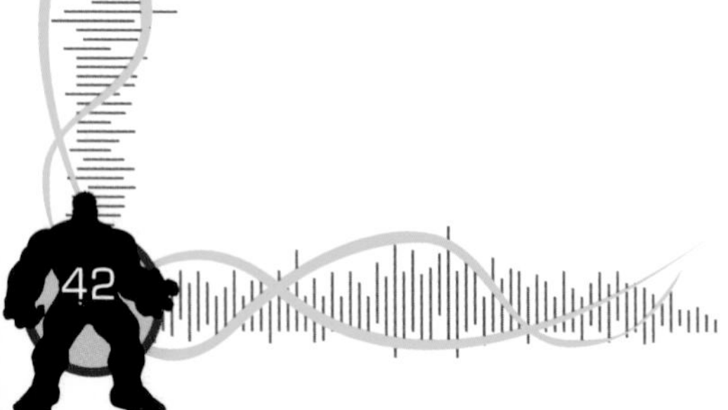

began firing, but the bullets couldn't pierce the green skin. The Hulk leaped toward the soldiers and threw them aside as if they were rag dolls.

The Hulk stopped for a moment and sniffed the air. Then, as if he sensed danger elsewhere, he leaped off into the night.

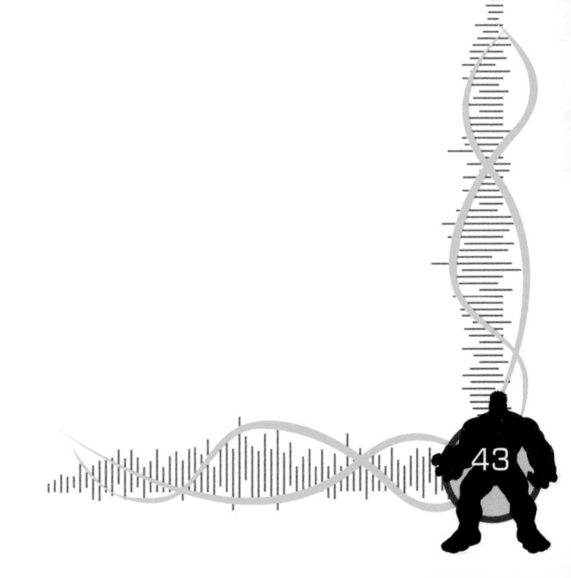

Attack of the Hulk-Dogs

Betty heard a rustling sound outside her forest cabin. She grabbed a flashlight and nervously stepped out the front door.

"Hello?" she called. Betty shined her flashlight around the yard—nothing unusual. As she turned to go back into the house, she saw it—a massive green monster with glowing eyes!

Betty started to run but slipped. As she was falling, the Hulk caught her in his green arms.

The Hulk gently lifted Betty and placed her on top of her car. For a moment they were face to face. Suddenly the Hulk sensed something amiss. Something was approaching in the darkness.

The horrible Hulk-Dogs, mutated by Bruce's father, bolted from the woods and leaped at the Hulk and Betty.

The Hulk opened the car door and placed Betty

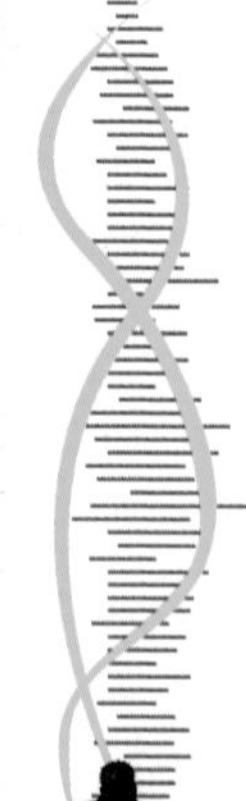

inside, where she would be safe. Then he turned to battle the Hulk-Dogs.

All three dogs attacked at once. The Hulk jumped straight up over the trees. As quickly as he had disappeared, he fell from the sky and landed on one of the Hulk-Dog's backs.

The remaining two Hulk-Dogs, still unafraid, charged at the Hulk. One clamped on to his ankle with its hideously sharp teeth while the other went straight for his neck!

Betty screamed. The dogs turned, and ran toward the car. One jumped onto the hood. It showed its sharp teeth and snapped its jaws at Betty. Huge paws clawed the windshield.

Just as the glass began cracking, an enormous tree came down on the second Hulk-Dog.

At the same time, the last mutant dog attacked the Hulk's neck. Its fangs clamped down but couldn't pierce his green skin. As the dog bit harder, the muscles in the Hulk's neck actually started to grow! As the muscle grew, it pushed out against the dog's fangs.

Before the dog could react, the Hulk reached down and smashed it. The Hulk-Dogs were through.

The Hulk was exhausted.

Then, without warning, the Hulk transformed back into Bruce Banner!

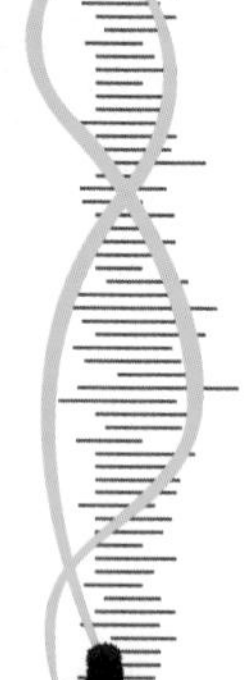

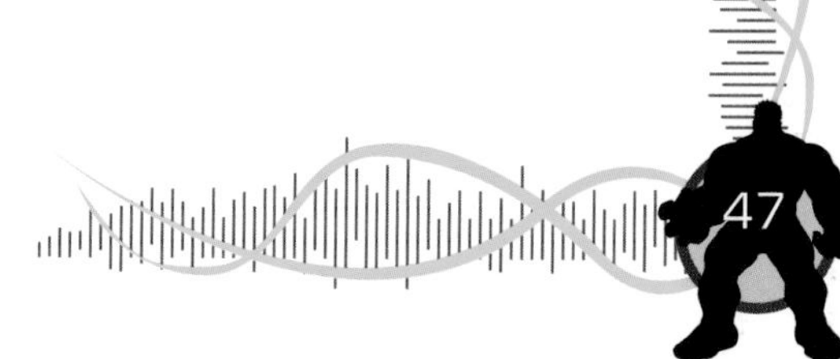

Captured

Betty called General Ross. "Dad, I'm scared," said Betty. "I . . . We need your help. I need to trust you." She hoped that her father could help save Bruce from his alter ego, the Hulk. She needed to buy some time to come up with a plan.

"Where are you?" asked General Ross.

"It's not Bruce's fault, you have to believe me," begged Betty. "His father, he tried to kill Bruce and me—"

Across the room, Bruce woke up. Betty quickly hung up the phone. She didn't want Bruce to hear her conversation.

* * *

Later that night, a strange noise came from outside. Bruce went to the window to investigate. *Pop!* A tranquilizer dart broke through the window and struck him in the stomach. Bruce immediately sank to the ground.

Betty ran to his side. "It's going to be all right," she said, trying to comfort him. "We're going

someplace safe, where no one can come after you." Betty had set up Bruce's capture for his own sake. She thought he would be safer where the Hulk could be contained.

The front door burst open and a military squad entered the cabin with weapons drawn.

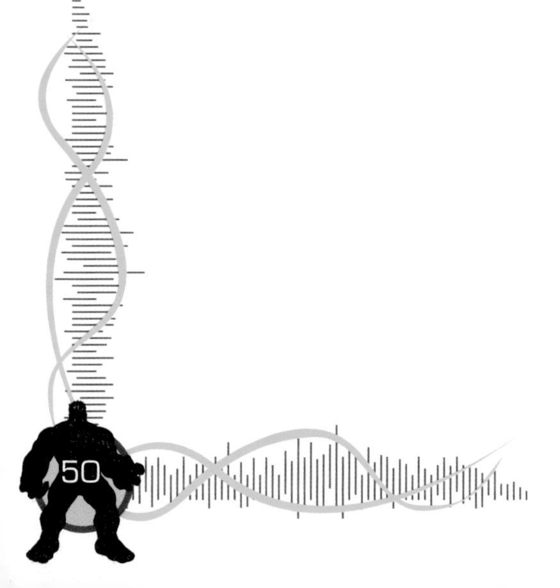

Home Sweet Home

Bruce was taken to a containment cell out in the desert. He had been returned to his childhood home—the Desert Base. Betty got permission to walk Bruce through the now abandoned town in hopes of jogging his memory. Even though Bruce had grown up there, he didn't recognize anything.

"I bet *it* remembers," said Bruce as he walked with Betty through the empty streets. "It must have been a child here too, inside of me. I feel him now, watching me, hating me."

"Hating you? Why?" Betty asked.

"Because he knows, one way or another, we're going to destroy him," Bruce replied.

As they walked, a particular house stood out to Bruce. He had the feeling he may have lived there. He entered the old, abandoned home.

Bruce froze. The room triggered repressed feelings of anger inside him.

"Why did you bring me here?" Bruce asked angrily. "What's the point of this? You saw what I am. You know as well as I do it's no use—I can't control the beast within."

"That's not true," Betty answered.

"It is true. C'mon," said Bruce, feeling very frustrated. "I'm supposed to have some sort of emotional breakthrough now? Reconnect with my inner child, exorcise my inner demons, find my true self, and everything will be just fine and dandy? Don't kid yourself," he said.

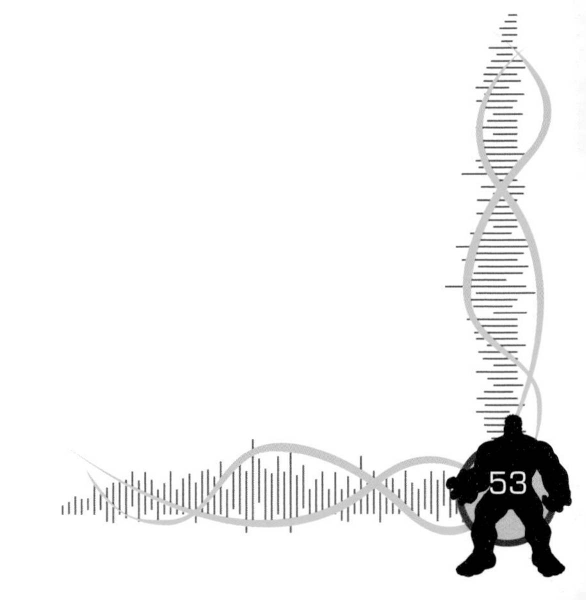

Greedy for Green

While Bruce returned to his containment cell, Betty went to the control room. But her access had been revoked. She wasn't allowed to enter the control room or have any contact with Bruce. She had been officially and abruptly removed from the project and was told to go home.

The government had turned over Bruce's case to Atheon, the company that Glen Talbot worked for. Wounded from their previous encounter, Talbot would finally have his shot at the Hulk. He wanted to harness the Hulk's strength and super-healing powers to make himself rich. He hoped to get millions for the technology.

In the containment cell, a number of small openings mechanically appeared in the walls. Red laser dots from guns covered Bruce. Any sign of the Hulk and they would blast him!

Talbot entered the cell with a metal walking stick.

"What are you doing here?" snapped Bruce.

"Good question. See, I need your cells to trigger some chemical distress signals—you know, so you can get a little green for me again," said Talbot smugly. "Then I'll carry off a piece of the real you, analyze it, patent it, and make a fortune. You mind?"

"I'll never let that happen," Bruce said.

"I'm not sure you have much of a choice," replied Talbot as he jabbed his walking stick into Bruce's stomach. It was really a stun gun! Bruce flew backward against the wall.

Feeling confident, Talbot went for Bruce again. This time he pummeled him with his fists. Talbot planted a left hook directly on Bruce's chin, knocking him out cold.

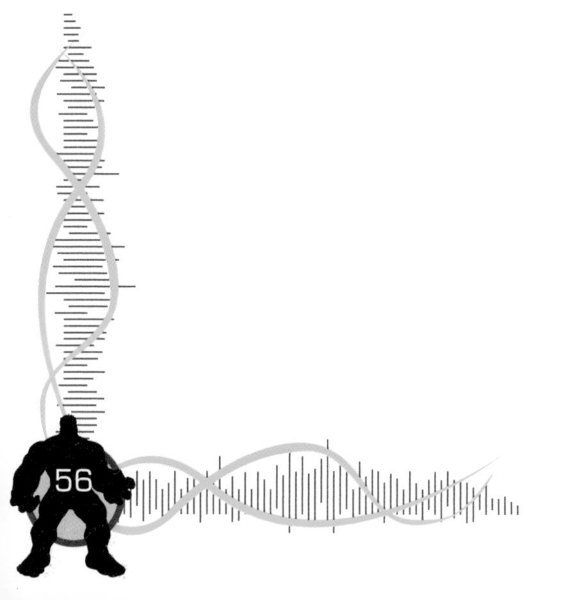

The Beast Is Back

Bruce, still unconscious, was now floating in an immersion tank. He was covered with wires and instruments.

Talbot was studying Bruce's brain activity. He was hoping to trigger a transformation into the Hulk.

"Let's fire up those brain waves, shall we?" ordered Talbot as he sent shocks through Bruce. As the waves surged through Bruce's body, his mind began to fill with painful images from his childhood.

At the same time, hundreds of miles away, David Banner was waiting for Betty to return home. This time he didn't want to hurt her; he needed her help. David was hoping to get Betty to set up a meeting for him with Bruce. But first he had to make her trust him.

When Betty arrived, David began to tell her his entire story. He told her how he had performed an experiment on himself, and how Bruce was the one

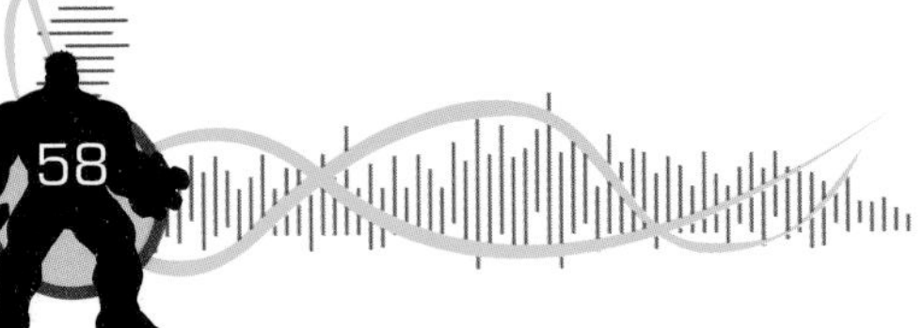

to suffer the consequences.

"I could feel it from the moment my wife, Edith, conceived—it wasn't a son I had given her, but a monster," he confessed. "If I could just make this one mistake go away, I'd give up everything, even my work.

"I remember that day so well," he continued. "I felt the handle of the knife, but she surprised me. It was as if she and the knife merged into one thing."

David Banner had planned on killing Bruce. But Bruce's mother stepped in front of the knife and saved Bruce's life!

Back in the immersion tank, it was almost as if Bruce could hear his father's words. The images flew across his mind. The young boy, the desert house, a fight between his parents, and then that horrible scream—the scream that had haunted him his entire life. Finally he knew his past. His father had killed his mother as she tried to save him!

It had been so terrible he had blocked it out.

The memories were too much. Bruce began to tense and shake. Once again his body was transforming. His muscles bulged, his skin turned green, and finally . . . the beast emerged. Half-man. Half-monster. The mighty Hulk thundered out of the darkness of Bruce's mind!

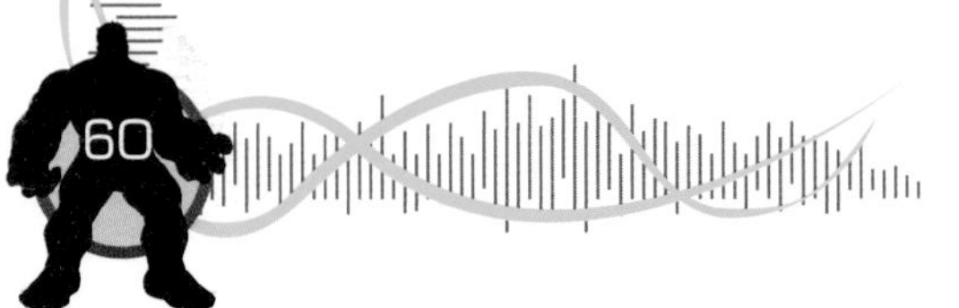

The Escape

CRASH! The Hulk smashed through the glass tank and emerged, huge and green, on the cell floor.

As he pounded on the cell walls, gas poured in from the walls. The gas was supposed to put him to sleep. It didn't work. Instead the Hulk ripped through the cell wall and stomped into the hallway.

"Nonlethals only," demanded Talbot. "I must get a sample of him. Hit him with the foam!" The Hulk would be useless to Talbot dead.

One of the techs stepped forward with a large-barreled gun and fired at the Hulk. A stream of sticky foam shot out of the gun, covering the Hulk. He was trapped!

As the Hulk struggled against the foam, General Ross found out what was happening and ordered a complete evacuation of the Desert Base. But Talbot ignored the general's orders and issued an order of his own—complete lockdown. The Hulk was not going to get away from him this time.

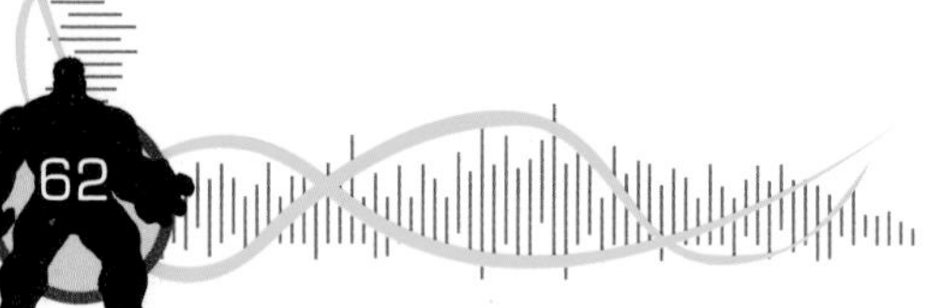

The Hulk continued to struggle against the sticky foam. "Let's get a sample of him," said Talbot as he cautiously approached the thrashing green beast. He took a laser drill and punched it into the Hulk's neck! The Hulk let out a deafening scream! With superhuman power, the Hulk released himself from the foam and pushed Talbot aside. He began to chase after his assailants.

Talbot grabbed a huge gun and stood directly in the Hulk's path. Talbot and the Hulk locked glares. The Hulk snarled, and before Talbot's eyes, he grew even larger! He grew so huge that he filled the entire underground tunnel!

Talbot fired at the Hulk, but the bullets bounced right off the thick green skin. They ricocheted off the walls and hit Talbot. He fell down, dead.

The Hulk crashed into the main hallway as General Ross took command of the situation. He ordered the troops to ready the strobe lights.

The troops put on their goggles and turned on the strobe. The Hulk threw his hands up to cover his eyes, stumbling back into the tunnel. He couldn't see anything.

Another group of soldiers shot huge nets at the Hulk, hoping to trap him. But he grabbed the nets and threw them back at the men. Then he destroyed the strobe light array with one pound of his fist.

The Hulk saw a sliver of daylight through the roof of the tunnel. He jumped up toward the light.

General Ross started to panic. He ordered the use of all weapons. He was going to make sure the Hulk was destroyed by any means necessary!

The weapons were useless. The Hulk had made it outside and into the abandoned neighborhood. Missiles began to explode all around him.

General Ross ordered Black Hawk helicopters to the area to drop bombs on the Hulk. They weren't fast enough.

As he looked out at the desert, General Ross caught a last glimpse of green disappearing into the horizon. The Hulk was gone. He may have escaped this time, but the road ahead would be difficult. It's impossible to hide when you're the most powerful creature on the face of the earth—the Hulk!